EEK!
Stories to make you shriek™

For Beginning Readers
Ages 6-8

This series of spooky stories has been created especially for beginning readers—children in first and second grades who are developing their reading skills.

How do these books help children learn to read?

- Kids love creepy stories and these stories are true page-turners (but never too scary).
- The sentences are short.
- The words are simple and repeated often in the story.
- The type is large with lots of room between words and lines.
- Full-color pictures on every page act as visual "clues" to help children figure out the words on the page.

Once children have read one story, they'll be asking for more!

For Eliza—D.A.

For my grandson, Ian Miller—J.S.

Library of Congress Cataloging-in-Publication Data

Anastasio, Dina.
    Fly trap / by Dina Anastasio ; illustrated by Jerry Smath.
       p.   cm. — (Eek! Stories to make you shriek)
    Summary: A fly trap plant, a seemingly innocent birthday present from Aunt Sarah, becomes a problem when it develops a craving for larger forms of life.
    [1. Venus's flytrap—Fiction.   2. Carnivorous plants—Fiction.
3. Horror stories.]   I. Smath, Jerry, ill. II. Title.
III. Series.
PZ7.A5185Fn   1997
[E]—dc20   96-16294
                                                  CIP
ISBN 0-448-41582-8 (GB)   A B C D E F G H I J   AC
ISBN 0-448-41557-7 (pb)   A B C D E F G H I J

EEK!

Stories to make you shriek ™

Fly Trap

By Dina Anastasio
Illustrated by Jerry Smath

Grosset & Dunlap • New York

It all started on my birthday.

Every year I have a party.

Every year my friends come.

Buddy comes too.

Buddy lives next door.

Buddy is a pain.

But Mom makes me ask him.

This year, Aunt Sarah was there.

Aunt Sarah goes all over the world.

And she always gives

the best birthday presents.

One year she gave me
a puppet from China.
Last year I got
drums from Africa.

This year she gave me a plant.

A plant?

"This is not just any plant,"
Aunt Sarah said.

"This is a fly trap."

"Oh," I said.

"It eats bugs," she said.

"OH!" I said.

"That's the dumbest present

I ever saw," Buddy said.

Like I said, Buddy is a pain.

Just then a little fly

buzzed by.

"Watch," my aunt said.

We all watched.

BUZZ, BUZZ, BUZZ.

The little fly buzzed

over to the plant.

The plant opened

its little jaws.

BUZZ!

The fly flew in.

SNAP!

The jaws slammed shut.

No more fly!

"Wow!" said everybody—

everybody but Buddy.

"It's still a dumb present,"

Buddy said.

Aunt Sarah smiled.

"Your plant is easy

to take care of," she told me.

"Just put it outside.

It feeds itself.

"But there is one rule

you must never break.

Never, ever feed meat

to the plant.

If you do . . ."

HONK, HONK.

A car horn was honking.

"Oh, my," said Aunt Sarah.

"That is my ride.

I am flying to Bora Bora tonight.

Happy birthday."

And Aunt Sarah was gone.

Buddy came over the next day.

I was outside with my plant.

Buddy was eating a hot dog.

And he was carrying a snake.

A big snake.

It even had a leash.

"Check it out," Buddy said.

"This is a <u>real</u> present!

My dad just gave it to me.

And it's not even my birthday."

Boy, is Buddy a pain!

Buddy walked over to the plant.

He watched it eat a big, black fly.

"Flies! Aren't you sick of eating flies?"

Buddy said to the plant.

"Here! Have a little hot dog."

Buddy tossed some hot dog to the plant.

"NO!" I yelled.

But I was too late.

SNAP!

No more hot dog!

My aunt had said,

"Never, ever feed meat to the plant.

If you do . . ."

If you do . . . what?

Aunt Sarah never said.

Well, now I would find out.

That night, we had a cookout.

My dad was cooking burgers.

They were thick and round.

Yum!

I looked over at my plant.

Its little jaws opened and closed.

Was the plant hungry too?

23

Dad and I went in to get plates.

We came back a minute later.

Something was wrong.

"That's funny," my dad said.

"I know I put six burgers

on the grill.

And now there are five."

I did not say anything.

I looked at the plant.

Funny.

It did not look hungry now.

The next morning,

I put birdseed in the bird feeder.

It is my job.

There are always lots of birds.

But not that day.

There were no birds at all.

Just a lot of feathers.

I bent down to pick one up.

SNAP!

OW!

What was that?

I turned around.

The plant bit me!

I thought about the plant
all day at school.

Aunt Sarah was right.

It was <u>not</u> just any plant.

And it was starting to scare me.

My mom was in the yard
when I got home.

She pointed to the plant.

"That thing looks more
like a <u>bear</u> trap
than a <u>fly</u> trap," she said.

She was right.

The plant <u>was</u> bigger.

Something was wrong.

"Keep away from that plant, Mom,"
I said.

Then I ran inside.

I called Aunt Sarah.

"I'm in Bora Bora.

Leave a message. I will call back,"

her machine said.

"Hey, Aunt Sarah," I said.

"Call me! Please!

What happens if you feed

meat to the fly trap?

I need to know!"

I sat by the phone.

I waited and waited.

A little later, the doorbell rang.

DING-DONG.

It was Buddy.

Boy, was he mad!

"Give me back my snake!" he shouted.

"I saw it go under your fence!

And I want it back!"

I did not want to go outside.

But I helped Buddy look

for his snake.

I had a funny feeling

that I knew where it was.

We looked and looked.

No snake.

Then we saw the leash.

It was on the ground.

It was right next to the plant.

"What happened to your plant?

It's so big!"

said Buddy.

I did not answer.

RING, RING.

The phone was ringing.

I ran to get it.

Yes! It was Aunt Sarah.

"I got your message, dear,"

she said.

"I have to make this quick.

The answer is—

if you feed meat to the fly trap,

it will want more, and more, and more."

Yes! It was true!

It all came together.

The burger.

The birds.

Buddy's snake.

All meat!

All gone!

Ever since Buddy fed the plant

his hot dog.

It had even tried to bite me!

What would the hungry plant

want next?

I looked out the window.

Buddy was next to the plant.

The plant's jaws were opening.

BUDDY!

"I gotta go!" I told Aunt Sarah.

I ran outside.

"Buddy! Get away from the plant!"

I yelled.

Of course he did not listen.

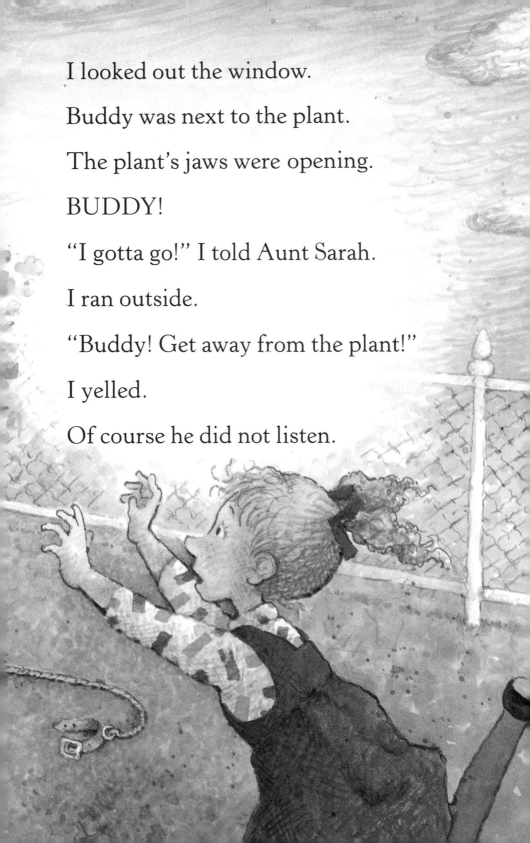

I had no time to lose.

I grabbed my mother's clippers.

"Out of my way, Buddy!" I yelled.

I ran over to the plant.

SNIP!

"Hey!" Buddy cried.

"Watch it! You almost got me!"

SNIP! SNIP! SNIP!

I chopped down

the hungry plant.

Soon it was just a big stick.

I was still holding the clippers.

Buddy stared at me.

He backed away.

"You must be crazy," he said.

"Crazy, crazy, crazy!

You just killed your new plant.

And you almost clipped me!"

Was I crazy?

Or had I just saved Buddy's life?

Who knows?

But I do know this—

Buddy never bugs me anymore!